NATASHA WING'S
The Night Before
the Wedding

Grosset & Dunlap

To my husband, Dan—NW

To Elise, Princess Bride of 2020—AW

GROSSET & DUNLAP
An Imprint of Penguin Random House LLC, New York

Visit us online at www.penguinrandomhouse.com.

Library of Congress Cataloging-in-Publication Data is available upon request.

ISBN 9781524793272   10 9 8 7 6 5 4 3 2 1

NATASHA WING'S
The Night Before
the Wedding

By Natasha Wing

Illustrated by Amy Wummer

Grosset & Dunlap

'Twas the night before the wedding
when at rehearsal dinner,
Dad and Mom said their daughter
had picked a true winner.

My sister's fiancé
was as nervous as could be.
But he gave a sweet toast
to his future wife—and me!

Jack's the ring bearer,
and I'm the flower girl.
I get to wear a pretty dress
that poofs when I twirl.

We practiced the ceremony.
I dropped pretend petals down!
But that ring bearer, Jack,
was being a clown.

Mom hung up my outfit
in the closet with care,
along with the glittery shoes
my feet soon would wear.

That night I nestled all snug in my bed,
while visions of flower girls danced in my head.

Early in the morning there arose such a clatter,
I sprang from my bed to see what was the matter.

Outside, it was raining.
My sister burst into tears.
"It's good luck," said my mother.
"It means many happy years."

The wedding planner came first.
Next the flowers arrived.

And look at that wedding cake!
Thank goodness it survived.

The wedding party got ready.
Everyone looked their best.
"Let's go," Mom told me.
"You and I must get dressed."

I slipped on my dress—
so pretty and pink!
And the wreath on my head—
so lovely, I think!

"Oh no!" I exclaimed
as I searched all around.

My flower-girl basket
was nowhere to be found.

Everyone pitched in
and looked high and low.

That wasn't the only thing missing.
Where was our dog, Bo?

When what to our befuddled eyes should appear,
but goofy lil' Bo running toward us in high gear!
His eyes—so wide! His ears—good grief!
He was holding my basket tight in his teeth!

The basket was shredded.
"Now what'll I do?"
"Use my purse," said my sister.
"It'll hold petals, too."

Yay! I filled up the purse
and hid it away,
so that Bo couldn't get into
more trouble today.

Then shortly before
the wedding was to begin,
the clouds drifted away.
The sun came shining in.

Voilà—the ceremony started!
It was like a parade!

There were fancy-dressed groomsmen
and a bunch of bridesmaids.

At last, it was my turn!
I skipped down the aisle.
On everyone's face,
I saw a big smile.

The wedding march played—
here comes the bride!
My sister looked like a princess
as Dad walked by her side.

The bride and the groom
both spoke from the heart.
They'll love each other forever
and never, ever part.

Jack held out the pillow,
and lo and behold!
Tied to the top
were two rings of gold.

When the bride and groom kissed,
we burst out in cheers!
Then my mom and my dad
wiped away happy tears.

The photographer took photos
with the tall ones in back.
Then she took extras
of me, Bo, and Jack.

I danced at the party
with my tall cousin Ross.
A bridesmaid caught the bouquet
during the toss.

I ate yummy foods—
as much as I could take.
But the best part of all
was the sweet wedding cake!

Jack chased me around
the long buffet table.
I escaped when I hid
behind my aunt Mabel.

I managed to stay up.
It took all my might.
"Happily ever after to you,
and to all a good night!"